For Rebecca

LADYBIRD BOOKS, INC.
Auburn, Maine 04210 U.S.A.
© LADYBIRD BOOKS LTD 1989
Loughborough, Leicestershire, England

Printed in England

New Boots for Rabbit

By Lucille Hammond
Illustrated by Lucinda McQueen

Ladybird Books

One morning Rabbit looked outside and saw
that it was raining. He remembered his new boots,
and he hurried to put them on.

"It's raining out," said Rabbit to his mother.
"Let's go for a walk so I can wear my new boots."

But Rabbit's mother was busy, and she said,
"In a little while, Rabbit, when I finish my work."

So Rabbit began to play by himself, with
his new boots on.

"With these boots," he whispered, "I could walk into
a river and catch the biggest fish in the whole world."

And he pretended he was a fisherman pulling in
a huge fish.

Then Rabbit said to his mother,
"Is it time to go for a walk now?"

"Later," replied his mother,
because she was still busy.

So Rabbit played some more by himself.

"With these boots," he said, "I could be a sailor in a storm, traveling all over the world."

And he pretended he was in a boat, tossing on the sea.

When he finished playing, he called to his mother, "Are you ready yet?"

"Not quite," answered his mother.

One more time Rabbit went off to play.

"With these boots," he said, "I could be an explorer in the jungle."

And he imagined himself walking through a rain forest, discovering new insects and birds.

At last Rabbit heard his mother say, "Time to go now!"

So together Rabbit and his mother went out for a walk.

But what a surprise! The rain had stopped, and the sun was drying up the puddles. Rabbit was so disappointed and cross that he felt like crying. He had waited all that time to get his new boots wet, and now the sun was shining.

Rabbit and his mother kept on walking until
they reached the park. Rabbit began to feel better.
He and his mother could look at the fountain with the
little pool all around it, and that was always fun.

Suddenly someone shouted, "Oh, dear me, help!"

It was a fancy-dressed grownup, and her hat had
blown into the fountain.

"I'll get it," said Rabbit, and quickly he waded into the shallow water to rescue the hat.

"Oh, thank you," said the fancy-dressed grownup when Rabbit returned the hat. "How lucky that you were wearing your boots." She smiled at Rabbit. "With boots like those, maybe someday you'll be a fisherman, or a sailor, or even an explorer!"

On the way home Rabbit felt very pleased and proud, and he skipped along in his new wet boots. *With boots like these*, he thought, *who knows what might happen?*